Rainbow Children: Magical Movi...

Praise for *Rainbow Children: Magical Moving Stories*:

'Linda has created more than a delightful story for children with the tale of the *Rainbow Children*; she has brought the most ancient wisdom of the Vedas into a most accessible and easy to digest form … for all ages. De-mystifying hitherto esoteric knowledge, and bringing it into the everyday realm of common sense and practical life skills, Linda has opened for us a treasure trove. No matter our age, no matter the issue we are tackling or struggling with, the delicately drawn, magical Rainbow Children help us keep our feet on the ground and draw on the resources we all have inside.

More than a book for bedtime, more than a yoga or dance class source book, *Rainbow Children* offers a simple yet effective grounding tool for all those who seek to understand themselves and the situations they find themselves in. Complex emotions, lack of confidence, finding our voice, insecurity, learning to trust love, intuition, and our spirituality; Linda tackles each of these in a safe and down to earth fashion that takes them out of the sphere of overwhelming or difficult stuff and into the everyday world of the things we all deal with each and every day, teaching children, and indeed each of us, to remember that for every problem we face there is a simple answer inside, and endless support.

Linda has accomplished, with this enchantingly illustrated book, a thing several years ago, when I first qualified as a yoga teacher, I thought would be a long time in the coming.

Fairytale, positive fable, activity book, wisdom teaching, this book shows what centuries of religious teachings have failed to divulge; that the answer to our disconnect with ourselves, each other, and the world we live upon, lies simply in self knowledge, and that the path to that knowledge itself is remarkably accessible and straightforward.

My sincere wish is that *Rainbow Children* becomes a familiar addition to every child's bedroom, classroom, and library, and that Rainbow Children of all kinds come bursting out all over all of our lives. Thank you, Linda. What a gift.'

Stephanie Bradley *Dip Ed, Dip TEFLA, Dip Phil,* **Teacher, Writer, Storyteller** (www.storyweaving.co.uk)

'*Rainbow Children* is an inspired and lovely project which, as an ex-teacher of Infants, I can sense will have a great interest for and influence on children in need of a spiritual input and support.'

Ruth White, bestselling author of ***Working with your Chakras***

ISBN-13: 978-1479213726
ISBN-10: 1479213721

www.magicalmovingstories.com

Library of Congress Control Number: 2012912354

British Library Cataloguing in Publications Data
A CIP catalogue record for this book is available from the British Library

Printed in the United States of America

Magical Moving Stories rev. date: 09/18/2012

~ This book is dedicated to the Earth and all of her children ~

~ May all beings have peace in their hearts, and may the
stories, songs, pictures, and ideas within this book
contribute in some way to the happiness
of all beings ~

~ With love ~

'One day, in the future, the animals will start to disappear.
People won't see wolves, bears, and eagles anymore.

The giant trees will disappear too. People will fight against
each other and won't love each other anymore.

The magnificent rainbow will erase slowly but certainly, and
people won't see any more of these.

And then children will come.

And those children will love the animals and will make the
animals come back.

They will love the trees and will make the giant trees come
back. And these children will love and will help the other
people to live in peace all together.

Those children will love the rainbow and will make it
reappear in the sky. It is for that reason that the Natives
have named these children The Rainbow Warriors.'

Anonymous (Native American Indians)

Contents

Acknowledgements

I would like to express my heartfelt gratitude to all of those who have supported and contributed to the development of *Rainbow Children* and these stories. In particular, I would like to express my thanks to the following:

- ≈ All of the children who I have shared *Rainbow Children* with and who have helped to shape these stories and illustrations, particularly Cicely, Lauren, Poppy, Melody, and my own children, Oscar and Jonah.
- ≈ The staff, parents, and children at the Exeter Steiner School, whose enthusiasm, support, and involvement allowed *Rainbow Children* to grow from a small seed into a tree whose fruits now feed many. Particularly Adam Smale, not only for offering feedback and loving support but for his chalk drawings, so beautifully produced for our children, that offered the inspiration for how to best illustrate my stories so that they would be appealing to children and encourage their artistic endeavours. And particular thanks to Helen King and Sue Bell for their warm, cosy, inspiring, beautifully held toddler sessions, which brought out my inner child who could then produce this work for all children.
- ≈ Embercombe, including the friends, the land, the people, the experience, for the sense of connection and inspiration given to me. Particularly Tim 'Mac' Macartney and Jonathan Snell, whose coaching and guidance have contributed so greatly to my self-development and deepening connection to Self and Earth.
- ≈ Maggie Clark for sharing her peaceful summerhouse retreats with nourishing land, wisdom, advice, and friendship.
- ≈ My teachers William Wray, Matthew McNeill, Elizabeth Whiter, Paula Mayura, and Ruth Noble, who have all helped to shape me, inspired me, and helped me along my journey to developing this project and these stories.
- ≈ Anodea Judith, whose book *Eastern Body, Western Mind* has been integral to my self development and learning and Jewels Wingfield who inspired my journey into ecstatic dance.
- ≈ My friends and colleagues, Gavin Frank and Christoffer de Graal, for believing in me, advising me, and co-creating beautiful songs and music to go with the stories.
- ≈ My spiritual sisters and friends, particularly Lucy Ananda, Inma Adarves, Catherine Johns, Helen King, Agata Krajewska, Fiona Maxwell, Terri Miranda, Melanie Philip, Nik Pitcher and Sara Verrall whose support, love, and honouring in so many different ways has allowed this to happen.
- ≈ Vincent Rymer, an artist of life, for bringing me colour, freedom, love, and joy.
- ≈ Timothy Slade and Justin and Jen Schamotta, whose support of Jonah and Oscar made this journey of emerging and creation possible.

~ And most of all, my unending gratitude to Mum and Dad,
the wind beneath my wings ~

Foreword

It was a pleasure and a gift to have Linda Ananda in my first intake of students for the Mayura Yoga School. Linda has become a unique and creative teacher; she is also a valued co-worker and friend. Her experience, intuition, and special *Mother Earth* quality was evident from our first meeting. It is with heartfelt delight that I accept the invitation to write this foreword as my contribution to sending *Rainbow Children* out into the world to be discovered and enjoyed.

Rainbow Children brings together a unique combination of yoga, dance, song, storytelling, and pure human fun to effortlessly reveal the wisdom of ancient teachings, encouraging children to discover their true nature and personal power from which to develop their ability to navigate life.

Each character brings to life a certain aspect of our experience and shows children that they don't need to be afraid of life's challenges but to see them as opportunities to find their inner resources and rise above them. For example, Mulad reminds us of our connection to the Earth, the element that links us to our roots, security, and groundedness. Tana teaches how to let go, to go with the flow and natural rhythm of life within the day-to-day things that happen around us and the feelings that they bring up. Mani chooses *right action,* which is cleverly exampled in Linda's story writing that characterises this aspect of human experience. These and more characters are brought to life by Linda's beautiful illustrations.

This is a unique work, introducing qualities of acceptance and adaptability that can elude the best of us in challenging times. How wonderful to learn these strengths through activity, stories, and fun as a child. I still remember very vividly the morals written within a couple of stories I was read as a child, and their messages have stayed with me into adult life.

Every encounter, friendship, or experience leaves its mark, and in a world full of fast activity bombarding our senses, much interaction with computers, and highly stimulating children's games, there is little time set aside for digesting or reflecting on real feelings and life issues. Linda's books are gems amongst the chaos, offering children the opportunity to recognise their own feelings and to see ways in which to deal with them towards the most positive outcome.

Rarely has a modern-day author attempted to incorporate the ancient teachings of yoga and its subtle body energy system of the chakras and brought it to life in an age-appropriate way for children of the world to understand and embrace.

Rich are the possibilities of a person whose awareness is awakened to these philosophies in childhood. Simple and obvious as they are in hindsight, so many of us are not able to navigate the complexities of our feelings with ease. These books could make that difference.

Paula Mayura
Founder of the Mayura Yoga School

Guidance for Teachers and Parents

Introduction

The *Rainbow Children* stories and activity format form a treasure trove for all those working with and connecting with children aged two to eleven, and those of us who are somewhat older but still connect to their inner children! These include parents, schoolteachers, teaching assistants, and those supporting people with special needs. The stories and activities are suitable for those with no experience of teaching movement, yoga, or dance and are also aimed at yoga and dance teachers.* (See note at end of this section.)

I have been teaching *Rainbow Children* for a number of years to a variety of different age groups, adapting the activities and stories to suit the understanding of the age range I am teaching. The stories are a culmination of many years of teaching and studying Eastern and Western philosophy, psychology, yoga, dance, movement, the energy body, and healing, and they came from the recognition of a need to portray the wisdom within all of these in a way that children can enjoy, digest, and utilise.

The stories and characters, along with the movement activities, bring balance and give children the inner resources to deal with life's challenges. The songs are not only beautiful but are affirmations and create a positive outlook and increase self-esteem.** (See note.) The illustrations are soft and drawn in a childlike way so that children can relate to them and are both encouraged and inspired artistically.

How to Use the Book

The first story, *Journey to the Light*, introduces the characters and brings a sense of balance; the following stories address these challenges:

Mulad's New Home - Moving home or starting school/dealing with life changes/feeling secure.

Tana's Heavy Load - Recognising and processing feelings/dealing with others' feelings/feeling supported/ emotional intelligence/allowing life to flow.

Mani's Fierce Fire - Managing the will forces/power and strength versus anger and force/dealing with anger and fiery tempers in positive ways/taking positive action.

Ana's Robin - Attachment/loneliness/the nature of love/loving yourself.

Vishud Lost Words - Speaking out/finding your voice/understanding yourself/speaking your truth.

Aja's Misty Mountain - Presence (being in the present moment)/clearing the mind/letting go of thoughts and negative thought patterns/creating a positive world by thinking positive thoughts/opening to innate inner wisdom.

Hasra's Connection - A sense of connection and interdependence/acceptance of the life-death cycle/ understanding of the elements and how we embody these/connection to *self* and *nature*.

There are many ways to utilise these stories in many different settings. In the home, it can be a connecting activity for parents and children. This could be a simple story time or playtime acting out of the story with movement and/or dance or putting on a simple puppet show using dolls. Parents can ask children to choose a colour and use the story with that colour in the title, or the parent can pick a story that suits a particular challenge that the child is currently facing. (Recordings of the songs in the book are available from the website.**)

Within the classroom, the stories can be integrated into the provision for self-esteem enhancement and personal development, such as SEAL, PSHE, or circle time.

The stories with the movement, dance, and yoga activities can be an interesting and holistic approach to physical education classes. (Many *Rainbow Children*-registered teachers offer classes within schools.*) Christoffer de Graal has developed specific music for each character, and it can be downloaded from the website. There you can also find playlists for other suitable music to use during the dance/movement elements.**

The stories and activities work extremely well within a drama lesson where there can be a focus on acting the story through movement and expression of the emotions involved within the story. Within the activities suggested, there are suggestions for pair and group work, trust building exercises, breathing and visualisation exercises, relaxation, and voice work, which the teacher can expand on creatively. The stories can be acted out with the children taking on the parts of the characters; simple costumes can be made or purchased.

The illustrations are a resource in art lessons, as they are drawn in a style that children can emulate and they can encourage the children's self-expression and self-belief.

Postures, Breathing, Movement, Visualisations, and Relaxation

I start each session by asking the children (in turn) to look inside and make a shape or do a movement to express how they are feeling. The group (or parent) should then copy this movement, reflecting it back to the child and creating a sense of connection, of being seen and understood.

I utilise a simple prop to illustrate balance and the colours of the rainbow making up white light. I have a crystal in each colour of the rainbow and a white candle (or battery-operated T-light). After each character has arrived in the story and the movement and dance have been completed for that character, one of the children places that colour crystal by the candle. Once all of the crystals have been placed around the candle, at the end of the class, the candle can be lit or the light switched on.

There are two types of movement activity and teachers can utilise one type, both types, or simply tell the story; the first type is movement based on traditional yoga postures, which are illustrated with stick men within the story. These shapes and movements embody the element of the story that they are adjacent to and should be practised during the story. This has the most enjoyable and engaging effect and brings the story to life. Some of the illustrations have two men. One is the starting position and one is the finishing position.

Some of the stick men have a solid set of arms and a dotted set of arms—the solid set is the starting position and the dotted set is the position that the arms move into. Where the movement has specific breathing to go with the movement, an in-breath is indicated by this symbol   and an out-breath is indicated by this symbol

Where there is one stick man with two different positions illustrated by dotted lines, the symbols for the breath are indicated next to the arm positions. When a noise or affirmation is made on the out-breath, this is

indicated by the words or sound appearing next to the   symbol. When the movement is focussed on one leg, the movement should be done twice, once on each side. The stick men should be simple to follow, but a full guide to the postures, their names, and ideas for expansion and visualisations are available on the website.** The postures can be practised with or without a yoga mat. If using mats, I place these in a circle on one side of the room to allow space for the free-form movement/dance on the other side.

The second type of movement is indicated by this symbol   and the handwriting-style, coloured text. These movement activities are free-form movement or dance that embodies the aspect of the story on that page. (Sometimes props are indicated. You can find these cheaply in thrift stores/scrapstores, and links to suppliers are on the website** along with lists of suitable music for each page of the story.)

The   symbol denotes a song to be sung. Each story/character has its own song that encapsulates the qualities of the character and the personal strengths portrayed in the story. MP3s of the songs being sung both with and without music can be downloaded from the website**.

This illustration   indicates the final relaxation. The children all lie on their backs in a line on the floor (or on mats). A long rainbow silk or cloth can be wafted over the children—one child can help with this. The use of the cloth/silk is almost essential with smaller children to hold the attention/focus. Ask the children to breathe deeply into their bellies, and then speak this rainbow visualisation (or create another to your taste):

As you breathe deeply, I would like you to see or feel a purple light around the top of your head [pause], a deep midnight blue, indigo light around your forehead [pause], a sky-blue light around your throat [pause], a beautiful green light of love around your chest and heart [pause], a golden, sunshine-yellow light around your tummy [pause], a deep orange light around your hips [pause], and a ruby-red light from the base of your spine all the way down your legs to the soles of your feet. And as the red light travels through the bottom of your feet, it grows roots connecting you to Mother Earth, holding you safe and secure as you go about your day.

Notes

* Yoga and dance teachers wishing to offer the *Rainbow Children* stories/format within classes, workshops, and children's parties will need to undertake a specific training programme and obtain a licence. See www.magicalmovingstories.com for more details of the training and registered teachers in your area.

** Recordings of the songs within the book and links to all resources, such as music, songs, dolls, teaching picture cards and stands, affirmation cards, and crystal/candle sets, can be found at **www.magicalmovingstories.com.** There you will also find downloads of new stories and illustrations, teaching ideas, and unique ideas for seasonal celebrations.

Journey to the Light

Once upon a time, the world became very dark and the Rainbow Children knew they must once again journey to join together so that the light could return to the world ...

Mulad lives in a log cabin in a beautiful valley where he sings with the birds and runs with the wolves. Although he loves his home, he knows he must journey to bring his friends, the Rainbow Children, together again to restore the light to the Earth. The Earth is his home that supports and cares for him.

He looks at the trees as he walks, seeing how the roots go deep into the Earth, holding and feeding the tree so that its branches can reach up to the sky.

As he reaches the river, he finds his wooden canoe tied on the bank and sets off toward the sea to find Tana.

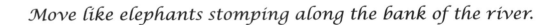

Move like elephants stomping along the bank of the river.

As he paddles the boat out into the sea, he starts to struggle against the waves, but soon he hears a voice gently calling him. It is Tana, a mermaid who lives in the sea. 'Hello, Tana,' says Mulad. 'Are you coming ashore?'

'I always wait for the tide to be moving towards the shore,' Tana replies, 'so that I can be carried to the land, going with the flow of the water.' As they wait for the waves to be going the right way, they play with the seals.

Tana loves to play with the seals and feels sad to leave them but so happy they are her friends. She experiences these feelings deeply and then lets them go, as if they are riding off on the next wave.

Dance like seaweed on a rock (feet planted firmly in one place on the floor, moving from hips, swirling and swaying with arms floating around) or in pairs: one pretends to be the water flowing around the seaweed. The seaweed's movement is in response to the movement of the water.

As they reach the beach, Mulad carries Tana in his strong arms to meet Mani.

Mani lives on the beach. He is a warrior of light and helps people to reach out for their dreams. He loves the sun and, in the late afternoon, when the sun starts to sink in the sky, he lights a big fire to keep everyone warm and to cook some beautiful food.

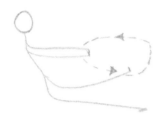

'What a beautiful fire!' says Tana. 'During a tree's life,' explains Mani, 'it has soaked up the sunshine through its leaves and has stored the sun's energy in its trunk. The tree then gives us back the light and warmth from the sun when we light a fire.'

As the fire grows, Mani feels the strength of his inner fire. He stretches his arms up in the air and shouts, 'I can do anything!'

One child stands in middle while holding red, yellow, and orange silk scarves—dancing like fire. When in a group, the other children dance around the fire in a circle—victory/ tribal dancing.

The smoke from the fire floats up into the air and Ana notices it. She looks down from her home in the apple tree to see the fire with Mulad, Tana, and Mani sitting around it. She knows she should now go and meet with her friends, and she is filled with love to share with them.

Her heart feels light, happy, and as if it is big enough to hold the whole world!

Her friend the robin flies with her down to the beach to meet the other Rainbow Children. They greet her with warm cuddles and big smiles.

Breathe in with hands in front of chest. Take arms out to the sides like wings whilst inhaling deeply. Repeat five times, visualising breathing in love and breathing out love. (A variation is to hug the body as the arms come in with the out breath)

Ana sends the robin to find Vishud. Vishud lives in the clouds. He is so light and airy that he can bounce from cloud to cloud. He loves to listen to the birds singing, and he helps people to sing and speak the truth, even when that can sometimes be difficult.

When Vishud sings, a beautiful blue bridge appears, linking the sky to the Earth. He travels down the bridge to meet his friends.

My words are strong and clear, my words are strong and clear.
I have no fear, I have no fear.
My words are strong and clear.

My voice is strong and clear, my voice is strong and clear.
I have no fear, I have no fear.

My voice is strong and clear.

The sky starts to turn from light blue to a deep, night blue. As the smoke from the fire curls higher and higher, it reaches the top of a majestic mountain—so high it is above the clouds. This is where Aja lives. She likes to be able to see a wide view, right across the horizon. When people need to see clearly, she brings them to the top of the mountain so that they can get a better view.

She sees the smoke and the little fire in the distance and trusts the feeling that she needs to go to the place where the fire is. She calls to her unicorn friend who carries her on her journey towards the fire and the other Rainbow Children.

Move like trotting unicorns (This can be done by cross crawling— lift right leg, bending knee, and touch knee with left hand. Then swap left leg/right hand. Repeat action whilst moving around the room.)

As Aja joins her friends, they all start to feel happy and peaceful now that they are together again. Stars appear in the night sky, and Aja and her friends look up to see if they can see Hasra.

Hasra lives on a star. Hasra loves stillness and pure white light and senses deeply the need to journey to the Earth to complete the rainbow that will bring back the white light to Earth.

Hasra waits very still and quiet, concentrating to see and feel for the next shooting star. Hasra travels on the star to the fire to complete the magical circle.

Dance with streamers like shooting stars.

15

As the Rainbow Children see Hasra, they are so happy to nearly all be together again that their colours glow brighter.

When they come together and join hands, a beautiful shaft of white light appears, joining the stars to the Earth. This lights up hearts all over the world and creates a feeling of bliss, peace, and harmony.

Mulad's New Home

The river near Mulad's cabin grows until the water covers his floors. Mulad leaves his home and finds a cave on the hill, where he decides to live.

He reminds himself how it takes a little time for a seed that falls in a new place to settle down, make roots, and grow into a beautiful tree, but he still feels sad.

Mulad starts to cry, and his tears flow down to the river. Tana, the mermaid, is swimming there. She knows that her friend is feeling sad and calls to him.

Mulad hears her call and walks down to meet her. Along the way, he soaks up the beauty of the valley and feels happier as he remembers that the whole valley is his home, not just one cabin or cave.

Moving as if stomping around the valley.

Tana is sitting on a rock by the river waiting for Mulad.

He carries her back to his cave. She suggests that they paint some beautiful, flowing pictures on the walls to remind Mulad of happy feelings.

Tana has some magical paintbrushes, and when they start to paint they are led by the paintbrushes around the wall in a flowing and joyful way to create wonderful colourful pictures.

 Dance holding a coloured silk, imaging you are being led by a magic paintbrush that is creating a beautiful, colourful picture of your dance.

Mulad does feel more joyful, but he still doesn't feel very brave and secure. Just then, their friend Mani arrives. Mani makes a beautiful fire in the middle of Mulad's cave, and they cook food in a pot for their dinner.

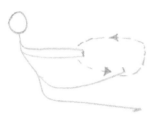

Mani spends some time reminding Mulad how courageous he is and how he has always looked after all of the creatures in the valley.

Mulad dances around the fire and shouts out, 'I am full of courage! I feel great!'

One child stands in middle while holding red, yellow, and orange silk scarves—dancing like fire. When in a group, the other children dance around the fire in a circle—victory/tribal dancing.

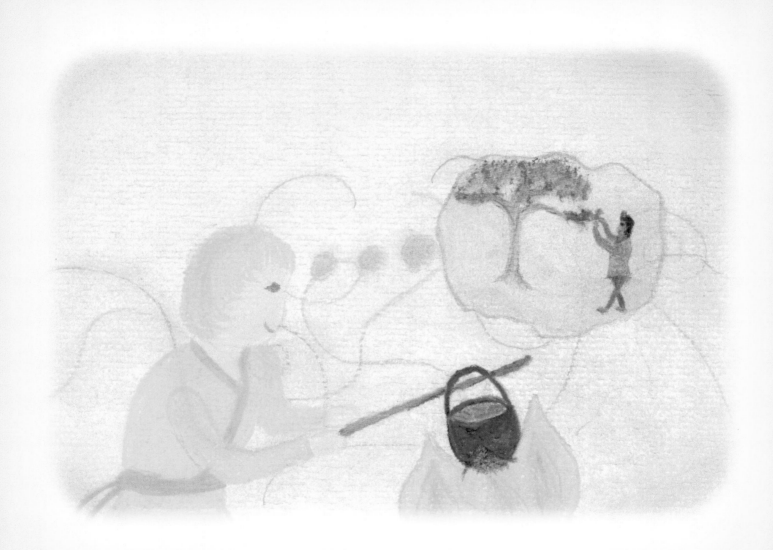

Mulad looks around his new home. Although he feels much happier and secure, the cave still doesn't feel like home.

They hear a tweeting noise and notice a little robin perched in the tree outside the cave. Their hearts lift as they realise that Ana is on her way.

Ana arrives and wants to make the cave feel cosy. She turns to her friend, the robin, and asks, 'Please, would you ask your friends to help by bringing some of Mulad's things from his cabin to the cave? That will help make it cosier for him.'

The birds bring lots of cushions, blankets, and sheepskin rugs into the cave, and Ana helps Mulad to make the cave cosy and full of loving feelings. It feels like she has given the cave a big hug.

Dance like flying birds. (If in pairs, carry a silk between the two.)

Vishud sees the birds flying to and fro from the cave and sings a beautiful song so that his blue bridge appears, linking his home in the clouds to the cave.

He tells Mulad how it might help him to feel at home if he talks or sings about all of the wonderful things he likes about it.

As Mulad sings, the blue bridge links Mulad's new home to the old cabin, and all of the safe, secure, and cosy feelings Mulad had there start to move across the bridge to his new home.

I am the Earth, I am the tree, and the roots go deep within me.
I am the Earth, I am the tree, and the roots go deep within me.
And my branches reach to the sky. I fly, I fly.
And my branches reach to the sky. I fly, I fly.

I feel the Earth beneath my feet, I feel the ground so strong. I belong, I belong.
I feel the Earth beneath my feet, I feel the ground so strong. I belong, I belong.

Heya heya hey, heya heya hey, heya heya hey ya ho.
Heya heya hey, heya heya hey, heya heya hey ya ho.

Aja is out riding on her beautiful unicorn and hears the singing. She rides over to the cave just as the sky is turning to the dark blue of night.

Mulad comes out of the cave to welcome her, and then they lie on their backs while looking up at the stars in the night sky. Aja points up and says, 'Mulad, look. All of the stars that shone over your cabin are also shining over your new cave.'

Dance/move as if moving/walking in space.

Up on one of the stars above their heads, Hasra sits and watches the friends looking up into the sky. Hasra's wings flap to increase the light energy.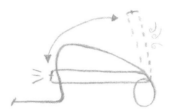

Then Hasra beams down white light from the star, until it surrounds Mulad's cave and all of the Rainbow Children with a beautiful, sparkly, protective bubble of white light.

Mulad feels safe, secure, and happy again, and his feelings move through all of the Rainbow Children. This makes their colours glow more brightly and the white light around them become even stronger.

Tana's Heavy Load

Tana has been so busy cleaning the sea and river of rubbish, and helping the seals and other friends, that she has not looked after herself and her own feelings.

Every time she has difficult feelings, she stuffs them into a bag that she carries on her back.

After a while, the bag gets so heavy that Tana can't swim anymore. She stops and cries.

Pretend to walk/dance with a heavy bag. The facilitator strikes a drum (or claps hands if a drum is not available) at intervals. Each time the children hear the sound, they pretend to stuff some more feelings into their bag, and their walking/dancing changes to represent it becoming even heavier.

Mulad is walking along the river's edge and sees Tana crying. He stops and helps her out of the river. They sit nice and still and open the bag together.

Some of the feelings are quite small, and as soon as they look at them, the feelings roll out of the bag and disappear into the ground.

Movement game: the facilitator stands at one end of the room with his or her back to the children. The children dance/move from crouched in a ball to getting bigger and bigger. When the facilitator turns to look at them, they twirl down and curl up in a ball on the ground. Once one of the dancers reaches the facilitator without being seen, the dancer takes the facilitator's place and the game starts again

Tana's bag feels much lighter and she tries to swim off, but she still cannot swim well with such a heavy load. Mani is looking out to the river's mouth and runs over to see if he can help Tana. He lights a warm fire so that they can sit a little longer.

Mani helps to open the bag and says, 'Tana, it is really great to help your friends and to look after nature, but you also need to relax sometimes and share the load so that you are being a good friend to yourself too.'

Tana starts to relax and thinks, *I deserve to relax and have special time for myself.*

Get into pairs. One sits and watches the other dancing like a flame with a silk scarf. Then swap over, observing the balance between activity and rest—receiving and giving.

Ana sees the smoke from Mani's fire and flies down with her robin to join them by the fire. She has a look in the bag and notices that lots of the feelings have been created by Tana looking after those that she loves.

Ana says, 'Tana, try not to feel so responsible for everyone you love. There is love all around us and all that you care about, and everyone has their own angel supporting and loving them. You have to take care of yourself to be able to help others.'

As Ana speaks, Tana feels the warmth of love all around her, like a soft, pink blanket.

Movement game: stuck in the love. The facilitator and children move like birds flying. When the facilitator touches a child on the shoulder, the child is stuck. One of the other children can free the stuck child by giving him or her a hug, visualising being the guiding angel and wrapping his or her wings around the other child.

Vishud looks down from his cloud and can see that he needs to help Tana with some of the bigger feelings in the bag. They are all tangled up in big balls.

He sings so that his blue bridge appears, linking his cloud to the Earth, and he slides down.

Vishud encourages Tana to talk about the big feelings, and, as she does, the tangled balls start to uncurl. Tana can see what they are about and what she can do. Vishud's support gives Tana the courage to speak the truth about how she feels.

Flowing water, gentle sea.
I hear the call within me.
I hear your call within me.

Flowing water, flowing sea, flowing water inside me.
Flowing water, flowing sea, wave of love inside of me.

Gentle mermaid, guiding sea,
I hear your call within me.
I hear your call within me.
Gentle mermaid, guiding sea, washing, cleaning, healing me.

Aja sees Vishud's bridge linking his cloud to the Earth and has a sense that she might be needed. She picks up her crystal ball and journeys down the mountain. Aja's crystal ball helps people to focus, to see clearly, and to create images with their minds.

When she arrives, Tana's bag is almost empty. As they look at the remaining feelings more clearly, they see that most of them don't belong to Tana! She has picked them up from other people!

Aja helps her to gaze into the crystal ball and visualise the people they belong to. Tana gently sends the feelings back to them.

Dance with rainbow streamers visualising sending feelings gently back where they belong.

Hasra looks down from the stars and sees one big ball left in the bag: Tana's biggest concern about how dirty the river and sea are getting. This is something Tana thinks about and helps to sort out every day.

Hasra sends down the white light to help support Tana and then travels down the shaft of light.

Hasra wraps his wings around Tana and says, 'Never forget, Tana, that there are always others to support us with things that seem too big for us to deal with alone.' Hasra promises to guide her to find a group that are working towards cleaner seas and rivers.

Once all of the feelings are out of the bag, Tana feels joyful, light, and free and can swim and play with the flow of life again.

Mani's Fierce Fire

Mani's fire has become fierce and strong. It keeps leaping up, and when it does, he feels angry and bossy.

He decides to put it out, but then he feels sad and bored and starts to mope around.

Moping style walking: head down, arms floppy, and feet heavy.

Mulad is out walking and bumps into Mani, who isn't looking where he is going!

'You look rather glum, Mani. Would you like to talk about it?' asks Mulad.

Mani replies, 'I'm having trouble with my fire. It gets so strong, and when it does I feel angry and I worry the fierce flames will burn my friends.'

Mulad reassures Mani. 'It is safe to light your fire. If you use it with care, your fire can help your friends.'

Mulad shares a story with Mani about a very helpful dragon. 'Everyone in the village was afraid of the dragon. Then one day, all of the fires in the village went out and the people were cold and hungry. The dragon went around to each home and relit the fires, and the people celebrated and lived happily with the dragon from that day on.'

 One child plays a dragon (costume, puppet, or imagination). The others stand still until the dragon comes and breathes fire on them. Then they dance like flames.

Mani walks on, imagining he is the dragon, until he reaches the sea and sees Tana.

Tana swims over to meet him and says, 'Hello, Mani. What are you doing?'

Mani tells her his troubles and Mulad's story about the dragon.

Tana reminds him that fire can also be used to burn away things that are trapping or blocking something. 'Do you remember the time that some seals were caught behind part of that old ship that got washed up in the river mouth? You helped to burn away the wood that was blocking their way so that they could be free and swim with the flow of water again.'

'Yes, I do!' exclaims Mani, feeling so much better about his strong fire and how it can be helpful.

Dance like seals swimming with the flow of water.

Now Mani is feeling a bit better. He sits and lights a little fire.

Ana sees the small wafts of smoke and flies down with her robin to be with him. 'Please, could you make your fire a bit bigger?' she asks. 'I can't feel it very much and would like to share all of the warmth and cosiness I feel with you when your fire is stronger.'

As his fire grows brighter and warmer, the friends bask in its warmth and sit and hug in its warm glow.

Movement game: stuck in the love. The facilitator and children move like birds flying. When the facilitator touches a child on the shoulder, the child is stuck. One of the other children can free the stuck child by giving him or her a hug, visualising hugging in the warm glow of the fire.

Vishud sees the friends by the fire and sings a strong song so that his blue bridge appears. He strides down the bridge to the fire.

The fire is still too small for Vishud to share it with them, so he asks, 'Mani, could you make a big, strong fire like you usually do?'

'The trouble is, Vishud, I worry that when the fire gets strong I start to feel angry,' says Mani sadly.

Vishud says, 'There are some ways to express angry feelings without hurting anyone else. Watch me!' Vishud starts to punch and kick into the air around him and talks gibberish in strong tones. Mani joins in and feels the tension leaving his body.

Once all of the angry feelings are out, they sing a song to celebrate the beauty of having a strong fire.

Fire warrior, fire warrior.
Fire warrior, fire warrior.

There's a fire burning inside of me.
It gives me strength and energy.
The sun is shining and I feel happy.
The warrior is leading me,
The warrior inside of me.

Warrior, warrior, warrior of light.
Warrior, warrior, warrior of light.

Aja arrives on her beautiful unicorn and asks, 'Mani, please, can you make your fire even brighter so that we can all see clearly?'

She takes out her crystal ball, and, as they gaze into it, they see images of all the people Mani has helped to keep warm and well fed with his fire.

Mani feels full of passion to offer his warmth and light to others.

Visualise holding inner light and then taking it out into the world.

Hasra sees the fire shining brightly once again and feels glad.

Hasra travels down on a star beam and says, 'Always remember, Mani, that our inner fire allows us to shine and that we each need to shine through our unique colours to bring light to the world.'

Mani feels very blessed to have his helpful, warm fire of light and his colours glow more brightly than they ever have before.

Dance with rainbow streamers, visualising taking own unique colours out into the world.

Ana's Robin

Ana's robin has flown away for springtime to make a nest, sit on her eggs, and hatch her babies. Ana feels sad and lonely without her most special friend.

Mulad comes walking across to Ana's tree and says, 'Hello, Ana. You look sad.'

'Yes, my robin has left to make her nest, and I feel so lonely without her,' says Ana.

'Always remember,' says Mulad, 'that Mother Earth and Father Sky are always there loving us

and giving us all we need. Come and lie down on the Earth with me ⌒───────⌐ and feel how really good it is to lie and roll on the ground and feel our Mother Earth holding us.'

Movement game: rolling around on the ground, really feeling the connection of the body with the Earth, the sensation in each part of the body as it presses against the ground.

They roll right down to the river, where Tana is waiting on a rock.

'Ana, you could let your feelings flow through you by crying the tears I can see in your eyes,' says Tana. 'Crying can feel really good, and it is OK to cry whenever we feel strong feelings of happiness or sadness.'

'Our tears that we cry take our feelings back to our Mother Earth and they dissolve … like a river rushing out into the great ocean.'

Ana feels relieved as the tears flow down her cheeks, dropping gently to the Earth.

 Hold hands and move like a river. And then make a circle, still holding hands, and move arms like waves in the sea. Finish by wiggling down to the ground like water dissolving into the Earth.

After Ana lets out her river of tears, she walks to the beach to meet Mani. As they sit by his warm fire, Ana feels the love inside her growing, and the love she has for herself takes away her feelings of loneliness.

Mani and Ana dance around the fire and shout out joyfully, 'I have so much love inside!'

One child dances like a fire with red, gold, and yellow silks. The other children pretend to dance around the fire.

Ana's heart is alight with love. Then she remembers that love is everywhere, in everything, even in the air that we breathe!

She blows some of her special bubbles to catch the love in the air. As they pop on Mani, he can feel the love inside them!

Dancing in a sea of bubbles. The children imagine that the bubbles are full of love and that, as the bubbles pop, the love goes inside them.

One of the bubbles floats all the way up to Vishud's cloud and  pops on his nose! He sings his beautiful song, and his blue bridge links his cloud to the beach.

Climbing down, he says, 'Ana, words can be like a bridge between two people – a bridge of love ... '

Ana sings a beautiful song of love for her robin. It drifts up to the tree where the robin sits in her nest, and Ana instantly feels connected with her again.

Love strong, love strong, open heart, love strong.
Love strong, love strong, open heart, love strong.

Endless beauty, eternal heart,
Hear my call, fairy heart.

Love strong, love strong, endless beauty, love strong.
Love strong, love strong, open heart, love strong.

Endless beauty, eternal heart,
Hear my call, fairy heart.

Love strong, love strong, open heart, love strong.

Aja hears the beautiful song of love and comes down from her mountain.

'That is a beautiful song, Ana,' says Aja. 'We can even send love when we can't speak to someone. Just by thinking loving thoughts of them, they will feel our love.'

Ana creates a strong image of the robin in her mind, whilst feeling love in her heart, and the feeling of connection grows even stronger.

The children create in their minds the image of someone they love, and then they send the person love. They can later ask the person if he or she felt it!

Hasra feels some of Ana's loving thoughts and zooms down on a star beam to Ana's side. Hasra takes her flying back to the apple tree where she lives.

Hasra picks an apple off the tree and then cuts around its middle. Hasra shows her the star there.

Looking up to the night sky, Hasra says, 'Just as the Universe is filled with stars and the apple holds a star at its centre, the Universe is filled with love, and you have love at your centre.'

 Dance with rainbow streamers or silks, visualising love circling all around.

Vishud's Lost Words

It is a dull day and all of the colour seems to have gone out of Vishud's world. The sea is grey, the sun has gone, and the mountains look bare and gloomy.

He cannot hear any of the beautiful sounds of birds singing, the wind in the trees, or water splashing in the streams. He tries to sing his beautiful song, but the words do not come out!

In his mind, Vishud asks for help. Suddenly, a beautiful bluebird flies down to Vishud's cloud and Vishud follows him. They swoop down to the Earth to find Mulad.

Mulad is out walking amongst the trees. just where he is. He hears a beautiful bird the trees above his head. He looks up and bit sad.

He is enjoying being singing up in one of sees Vishud looking a

Vishud signals that he has lost his words, and Mulad asks him to come down to the ground.

'Vishud, sometimes to find the right words and the strength to say them, we need to feel our connection to the Earth holding us,' says Mulad.

They plant their feet firmly on the ground, and then Mulad teaches Vishud a verse he says when he needs to feel strong: 'My feet are planted on the Earth; I feel so safe and strong. The warmth of love fills my heart; I know that I belong.'

As the Earth's energy spreads up their legs, filling them with strength, it also travels up the trunk of the tree. The bluebird starts to sing a joyful song, and beautiful leaves open on each branch.

Move like trees. Imagine how they might walk, so connected to the ground.

The bluebird flies on and Vishud follows. They come to the sea's edge where they can see Tana playing with some dolphins.

'Vishud, would you like to ride the waves with my dolphin friends and me?' asks Tana.

As they swim through the gentle flow of the waves, Vishud feels comfortable and relaxed, and he starts to notice his feelings flowing through him. It is as if his body is talking to him, and he listens very carefully … Just as Vishud starts to listen to himself, the bluebird flies down from the sky to land on the surface of the water.

The bird starts to sing a flowing melody and the clouds open, making the sea a beautiful, shining turquoise.

Dance, flowing like a river.

Tana swims with Vishud back to the water's edge, and the bluebird leads Vishud up the beach to meet Mani.

Mani is dancing by the fire, hoping for the sun to come out and warm the day. He notices that Vishud is not speaking.

Mani wants to help his friend to find his words and suggests, 'Sometimes I find it helps to move strongly to find my inner power and confidence. Would you like to try it?'

As they move together, Vishud starts to see what is right for him and who he really is. They stand like warriors and shout out, 'It feels good to be me!'

He feels the warmth inside of him reflecting the warmth of Mani's fire, and he feels more confident to find the words that reflect how he feels inside.

The bluebird flies down to rest on Vishud's shoulder and sings a joyful, playful tune. The clouds part even farther, and sunshine floods the beach with golden rays of light and warmth.

One child dances like a fire with red, yellow, gold, and yellow silks. The other children pretend to dance around the fire.

Vishud walks on towards Ana's apple tree while the bluebird flies above him. When they reach the tree, the bluebird flies up with Vishud to sit on the branch with Ana.

Although Vishud is feeling content, joyful, and confident, his words are still not flowing. Ana and Vishud breathe deeply together, which opens their hearts and helps them to relax. The words that Vishud needs to say start flowing into his mind from his heart.

As the bluebird feels the love flowing from Ana and Vishud, it starts to fly joyfully around the tree while chirruping its song. Pink blossoms open on the tree.

Use silks as wings. Fly and take beautifully decorated letters from a basket at one end of the room and place them in a nest of pink muslin at the other end. (You could prepare letters that spell out something appropriate, such as 'My words come from my heart.')

As the bird sings, Vishud feels his words of truth coming from his heart and they pour out of his mouth in a beautiful song …

His blue bridge appears, linking the tree to Aja's mountain where it still looks grey and bare.

My words are strong and clear.
My words are strong and clear.
I have no fear, I have no fear.
My words are strong and clear.

My voice is strong and clear.
My voice is strong and clear.
I have no fear , I have no fear.
My voice is strong and clear.

Vishud and the bluebird travel along the bridge while singing beautifully together.

As they climb the mountain, the rocks turn from grey to a beautiful purple as they touch them. As Vishud and the bluebird pass the bushes, leaves and flowers burst open at the sound of their song. More birds join them, and birdsong fills the air. As the bluebirds circle in the air, the sunshine starts to stream down, making everything golden. And as they fly over an opening in the rocks, a beautiful mountain stream gurgles into life, splashing happily down the slopes to meet the river.

Aja meets Vishud on the mountain path and carries him the rest of the way on her unicorn.

When they reach the top of the mountain, they can see clearly. Aja shows Vishud how the beautiful song of his heart has made the world look completely different. The world is full of colour and joy, and Vishud feels that he belongs.

As Vishud gazes out at the stunning view, a beautiful rainbow appears in sky.

Dance with rainbow streamers.

As the sun sets and the sky turns to an indigo blue, the friends look up at the stars. They see one star glow more brightly until its beams reach the top of the mountain. Hasra travels down the star beam to join them.

Hasra is very happy that Vishud has found his heart's song and says, 'Remember, Vishud, that you always have the support of your guiding angel, and if you ever need the courage to sing your heart song, you can stop, still and strong for a moment, breathe deeply, and feel angel's wings around your shoulders. The white light of the Universe will surround and protect you.'

Vishud feels happy and strong, knowing that he has found his heart's song and the courage to sing it to the world.

The one in front leans back into arms outstretched. The one partner with his or her arms arms. Breathe deeply and supported by your angel.

the support of the other with behind gently holds his or her underneath the partner's relax, visualising/feeling being

Aja's Misty Mountain

Aja usually has a clear mind and a clear view of what is happening. One morning she awakes and finds her mind is crowded with negative thoughts. She tries to find space by looking at her sweeping view, but her mountain is wrapped in mist. She climbs onto her unicorn and rides down the mountain to find some help.

Aja finds Mulad sitting on the ground under the trees. He is watching something intently.

Aja walks over to Mulad and says, 'Can you help? My mind is so busy, and I would like to find some calm again.'

Mulad replies, 'Lay down with me and look closely at nature. When I do  this, it helps me to be here and now, only in this moment, and I find that all thoughts simply disappear.'

Aja rests on the grass for a while with Mulad and enjoys watching all of the activity of the small creatures that she can see. All of her focus is on what she is watching, and her mind is able to rest.

Slither like snakes on the ground, getting close to the Earth.

Aja's mind feels clearer as she walks down to the sea. She sees Tana diving in the waves. It looks like fun, and she wades into the water to join her.

'Tana, my mind is so busy today,' says Aja.

Tana replies, 'To help our mind to stop talking so much, we can enjoy our body more and explore how we feel.'

Tana shows Aja how to do this by playing and diving in the waves. After playing in the water, Aja feels much fresher and more open.

 Dance like waves.

Aja walks out of the ocean and onto the beach where she decides to dry off by Mani's fire.

Her mind still seems to be creating negative thoughts, and she tells Mani, 'My mind isn't very clear today. It is less busy than it was earlier, but I am still having negative thoughts.'

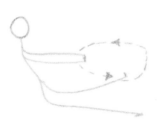

Mani says, 'The best way to clear the mind of negative thoughts is to cook up some nice juicy ones that we want!'

They *cook up* some wonderful, warm thoughts filled with light and joy, and then they dance around the fire while shouting, 'I create my world with my positive thoughts!'

One child dances like a fire with red, yellow, gold, and yellow silks. The other children pretend to dance around the fire.

Aja feels much more positive as she walks on but still looks rather preoccupied when she walks up to Ana's tree.

Ana calls down to her and sends her robin to guide Aja up to the branch where she is sitting.

'I'm feeling much more positive than I was earlier, Ana, but I'm still feeling rather disturbed by my thoughts,' says Aja.

Ana replies, 'I find it helps me when I breathe deeply, filling myself and my thoughts with love. I then breathe away any negative thoughts, seeing them in a beautiful, pink balloon and then letting them float away ... '

Breathe in with hands in front of chest, visualising filling thoughts with love. Then take arms straight up above the head with the out breath, visualising sending thoughts out into a pink balloon and letting them go.

A beautiful, pink balloon floats past Vishud's cloud. Vishud looks down and sees Aja waving to him.

He sings a beautiful song and his blue bridge appears, linking his cloud to the ground. Aja climbs the bridge to visit Vishud.

Vishud says, 'Is that pink balloon yours, Aja?'

'Yes, it is,' says Aja. 'It is carrying some of my negative thoughts, now filled with love, away on the breeze.'

Vishud replies, 'Sometimes I find that I simply need to say what needs to be said, so that I don't have to think about it anymore.'

Aja sings with Vishud, and the rest of her thoughts float away like clouds.

I climb to the top of the mountain and see clearly.
I climb to the top of the mountain and see clearly.

Clear sight, clear mind, open space, deep wisdom.
Clear sight, clear mind, open space, deep wisdom.

Climb to the top of your mountain and see-e-e-e.
Climb to the top of your mountain and see-e-e-e.

Aja's mind is clear again. She can focus on what is happening right now and fully enjoy all that is around her.

The mist clears from her mountain, and as the sun shines on the little patches of mist, it creates little rainbow clouds in the sky. She travels back to the top of the mountain.

Dance with rainbow streamers.

As the day ends and the stars appear, Hasra travels down on a beam of white starlight. Hasra listens to Aja's story and agrees that it is important to take space and time alone, with a clear mind. Then the space within the mind will create only beautiful thoughts that sparkle like stars.

Hasra turns to Aja and says, 'It is important to have this quiet space in your mind, because when your angel speaks to you, it is always in a whisper. And this can often seem like a thought. If our minds are busy with thoughts, we cannot hear the angels whisper.'

Sitting quietly with a partner sitting a little way away from you, see if you can hear your partner whisper a message.

Hasra's Connection

Hasra loves the white light energy and knows that everyone shares it. Hasra is connected to it and always says, 'The light is a part of me.'

Hasra wants to share this beautiful feeling of connection and let the other children know that the things they love the most are also a part of them. Hasra zooms down on a shaft of white light to visit the other Rainbow Children ...

Hasra finds Mulad dancing amongst the trees and asks him, 'What do you love most?'

'I love the Earth and feeling connected to Mother Earth,' replies Mulad.

Hasra says, 'You came from the Earth. Everything that exists does. The Earth truly is our Mother!'

Hasra shows Mulad how the plants grow from the Earth, eating from her goodness to form themselves. Then the animals and people eat the plants and form their bodies from the goodness in the plants. He says, 'When our bodies are old and worn out, they return to the Earth to become goodness that can form something else.'

They feel how the Earth within us helps us feel rooted, connected, and secure.

Repeat this sequence three to five times while visualising being a seed growing into a plant and then returning to the Earth, then becoming nourishment for something else to grow and growing up into a plant again …

Hasra walks to the ocean to find Tana. She is playing with the seals and swims over to sit on a rock and talk to Hasra.

Hasra says, 'Tana what do you love the most?'

Tana replies, 'I love to swim and play in the water. It makes me feel refreshed and relaxed.'

Hasra says, 'Three quarters of our bodies are made of water, and this keeps everything flowing and refreshes our insides!'

Hasra points to the waves and says, 'Underneath the waves, the sea is deep and calm. We can be like this, feeling big waves of emotion, whilst remaining calm deep down inside.'

They connect with the feeling of water inside and outside and feel how it makes them feel comfortable and relaxed. They discover that water is all about being easy ... With ease and flexibility, water flows into whatever container it is poured into.

 Dance being water. Hold hands in a long line and move around like a flowing river. Then everyone curls up into a tight spiral, as if the water has moved into a small pool, then out into a flowing river again, moving faster this time. Then everyone slides down onto the floor, limbs spread out and touching each other as if the water has moved into a large lake or the sea.

Hasra walks on up the beach to find Mani dancing around the fire. 'Mani, what do you love the most?'

Mani replies, 'I love fire: the warmth, the light, the way I can cook beautiful things to feed others with the fire.'

As he talks, the sun breaks through the clouds. Hasra points to the sun and then to the fire and says, 'The fire is a *little sun*. The trees soak up the sun's energy into their trunks and branches. Then, when we light the wood from the tree, it gives us back the light and warmth of the sun.'

Hasra says, 'We are also a *little sun*. We take energy from the plants that we eat, which are filled with the sun's energy. Then the fire in our tummies makes this into energy that we use to help others and create beauty, which is our way of giving the sun's light and warmth back to the world.'

Mani feels really positive and powerful and feels how our inner fire can fill us with warmth and joy.

They dance around the fire while singing, 'I am everything, and everything is in me!'

Dance in pairs. One dances like a fire around his or her partner with flame-coloured silks. The other does a dance in response to the fire, showing how he or she feels filled with joy and warmth.

Hasra flies to Ana's apple tree and sits with her in its branches. He asks, 'What do you love the most?'

'I love the air and moving and dancing in the air with my wings outstretched, soaring like a free bird,' says Ana. 'And I love breathing in the scent of the beautiful blossom that is carried on the breeze.'

Hasra says, 'The air inside us allows us to move. Did you know that we breathe in the air that the trees breathe out and that the trees breathe in the air that we breathe out? People need trees and the trees need us.'

They breathe the air deeply, exploring how breathing brings energy to their bodies and that love brings energy to their hearts. They realise that all people share the same air and share the same love.

Ana and Hasra discover that, by focussing on the air inside and outside, they can feel connected, feel free, and dance in love.

Sit back to back with a partner while holding hands. One bends forward and the other leans back. The one leaning forward breathes out, and the one leaning back breathes in, then they keep swapping slowly, breathing in and out deeply. They appreciate the sense of connection and how each person is giving support to, and receiving support from, the other.

Hasra flies up to the cloud where Vishud lives , even higher in the air where there are no solid forms.

Hasra asks Vishud, 'What do you love the most?'

Vishud replies, 'I love sound and to sing!'

Hasra says, 'Without the air within us, we wouldn't be able to think, talk, or sing. Air energises our minds, carries our sound out into the world, and brings all of the beautiful sounds from the world to us.'

They connect to the feeling of air and realise how this helps them fly above any limiting thoughts. When they sing their sounds out into the air, it really lifts them to a brighter and lighter feeling.

Angel flying high, golden wings in the sky.
Pure white light, star burning bri~i~i~i~ght.

Beautiful and true, peace and joy to you.
Pure, pure light, the stars are burning bright.

We are all one, spirit in the sun.
Pure white light, star burning bright.
Pure white light, star burning bright.

As they sing, Vishud's beautiful blue bridge appears, linking his cloud to the top of Aja's mountain. One end is light blue like the daytime sky, and the end touching the mountaintop is deep, indigo blue like the night sky.

Hasra crosses the bridge to Aja's side. Aja is gazing out at the early evening sky.

Hasra says, 'What do you love the most, Aja?'

Aja replies, 'I love the feeling of fresh openness that gazing into space gives me.'

Hasra explains. 'We are also filled with space inside. If we feel overcrowded or squashed by too many words, thoughts, noises, or people, we can just imagine a universe filled with stars inside of us. Then, however crowded the outside might seem, we can feel free and open inside.'

Aja feels content as she connects with the infinite space and a galaxy of sparkling white stars inside her.

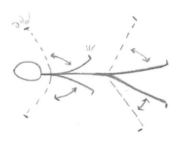

Lie on your back. Breathe in whilst moving arms and legs up and out to the sides, making a star shape with the body. Feel the extra space as you move the arms and legs up and out and breathe in. Visualise that space filling with a galaxy of stars.

Hasra keeps on looking out across the sky and the low evening sun. A light rain is falling from one of the clouds, and as the sun shines through the rain, a beautiful rainbow appears.

'Aja, each one of us is like a little raindrop with the light of the sun shining through it. We can see the one white light make many different rainbows, each one unique, special, and beautiful, with its own message for the world,' says Hasra.

'If you look very carefully, perhaps you may see these colours in soft clouds swirling around those you meet … '

 Dance with rainbow streamers.

Hasra is filled with love and joy, and he hears a lovely sound. As he listens carefully, he realises the sound is the song of the Universe, the *Uni-verse: one song*.

Play pentatonic lyre, glockenspiel, or thumb piano (Kalimba), and pass the instrument around to all of the children for them to play in turn.

Linda Ananda *MSc, DipM, DipCD, DipYT, DipHypCS, LHS, ATH* is a therapeutic healer specialising in movement and a teacher of dance, yoga and practical philosophy. Her journey has led her through an exploration of eastern and western wisdom and movement practices to a destination of presence, connection and blissful peace. Linda lives in Devon with her two children, Oscar and Jonah.

Gavin Frank is a Voice Facilitator, Singer and Musician. His background stems from choirboy to BA-Hons Music Degree through to Naked Voice training. He has 12 yrs voice experience; empowering people to express the full resonance and depth of their own voice. Gavin performs and records in the duo Madrum.

Printed in Great Britain
by Amazon